STORY OF SI GRAND BAZ

GUIDE BOOK

HATEM BRYAN MOHAMED
NEW 2025

STORY OF SEASONS: GRAND BAZAAR

GAME GUIDE:

Complete Guide and Walkthrough :Tips, Tricks, Strategies and Help

GUIDE BOOK

INTRODUCTION

Story of Seasons: Grand Bazaar – The Ultimate Game Guide

Your Complete Handbook for Farming Glory, True Love, and Marketplace Mastery in Zephyr Town

Welcome to Zephyr Town — a peaceful village full of charm, opportunity, and secrets waiting to be uncovered. In Story of Seasons: Grand Bazaar, your journey begins with a small plot of land and a big dream. With the right knowledge, you'll transform it into a thriving farm, win hearts, and become the star of the weekly bazaar.

This unofficial, all-in-one guide is your trusted companion on the road to farming greatness. Whether you're planting your very first turnip or looking to 100% the game, this book gives you a clear, actionable path to success. Expertly organized and easy to follow, it's designed for players who want to go beyond the basics and truly master every part of the game.

Inside, you'll unlock the full potential of your Zephyr Town life:

🌾 Farming Like a Pro – Learn optimal seasonal crop rotations, how to double-water for better yields, and how to maintain high ★ quality. Includes detailed charts on growth times, profits, and spoilage risks.

🐑 Animal Management & Pet Care – Discover how to care for cows, chickens, and sheep for maximum production. Includes tips on breeding, brushing routines, and unlocking barn upgrades and pet benefits.

🛠 Crafting & Windmill Secrets – Make the most of your harvests with full windmill recipes and tips for crafting perfume, jams, cloth, and more.

Learn the best production cycles for profit and efficiency.

💖 Love & Friendship – Win over every villager with gift guides, daily schedules, and heart event walkthroughs. Learn how to get married, start a family, and experience hidden romance scenes.

🎉 Festivals & Bazaar Domination – Outshine the competition with festival prep tips and judging criteria. Use weekly bazaar strategies to boost your sales, spot trends, and build a reputation.

📅 100% Completion Roadmap – A complete seasonal plan for unlocking tools, animals, and recipes. Includes collectible checklists, upgrade timelines, and post-game challenges.

Whether you're playing on a Nintendo DS or emulator, this guide helps you get the most out of every in-game day. With zero fluff and tons of practical advice, it's your ticket to a richer, more rewarding Zephyr Town experience.

🎯 Ready to take the bazaar by storm and live your dream farm life?

Grab your guide now and start building your legacy!

CONTENTS

CHAPTER 1: 18

    All Romance Options: Bachelors and Bachelorettes 18

    List of All Bachelors and Bachelorettes 19

    All Bachelors 19

    All Bachelorettes 21

    Which Character Do You Want to Date? 23

    Romance in Story of Seasons: Grand Bazaar 23

    Choose From 12 Romance Options 23

    Can You Marry the Same Gender? 24

    Raise Friendship Points to Romance 24

CHAPTER 2: 26

    Can You Marry the Same Gender? 26

    Can You Marry the Same Gender 26

    Yes, Same Gender Marriage is Allowed 26

    No Changes From Original Game 27

CHAPTER 3: 28

    List of All Characters 28

    All Characters 28

    List of Romanceable Characters 28

    List of Non-Romanceable Characters 30

CHAPTER 4: 33

STORY OF SEASONS: GRAND BAZAAR

Bachelors 33
Jules Character and Romance Details 33
Jules Character Information 34
Character Profile 34
Can You Romance Jules? 35
Will You Romance Jules? 35
Jules Character Preview 35
Jules Official Description 36
Derek Character and Romance Details 36
Derek Character Information 37
Character Profile 37
Can You Romance Derek? 38
Will You Romance Derek? 38
Derek Character Introduction 38
Derek Character Preview 39
Lloyd Character and Romance Details 39
Lloyd Character Information 40
Character Profile 40
Can You Romance Lloyd? 41
Will You Romance Lloyd? 42
Lloyd Character Introduction 42
Lloyd Character Preview 42
Lloyd Official Description 43
Gabriel Character and Romance Details 43

Gabriel Character Information 44

Character Profile 44

Can You Romance Gabriel? 45

Will You Romance Gabriel? 45

Gabriel Character Introduction 45

Gabriel Character Preview 46

Gabriel Official Description 46

Samir Character and Romance Details 46

Samir Character Information 47

Character Profile 47

Can You Romance Samir? 48

Will You Romance Samir? 49

Samir Character Introduction 49

Samir Character Preview 49

Samir Official Description 50

Arata Character and Romance Details 50

Arata Character Information 51

Character Profile 51

Can You Romance Arata? 52

Will You Romance Arata? 52

Arata Character Preview 52

CHAPTER 5: 54

  Bachelorettes 54

  Sophie Character and Romance Details 54

Sophie Character Information 54
Character Profile 54
Can You Romance Sophie? 56
Will You Romance Sophie? 56
Sophie Character Preview 56
June Character and Romance Details 57
June Character Information 57
Character Profile 57
Can You Romance June? 59
Will You Romance June? 59
June Character Preview 59
June Official Description 59
Freya Character and Romance Details 60
Freya Character Information 60
Character Profile 60
Can You Romance Freya? 61
Will You Romance Freya? 62
Freya Character Preview 62
Freya Official Description 62
Maple Character and Romance Details 62
Maple Character Information 63
Character Profile 63
Can You Romance Maple? 64
Will You Romance Maple? 65

Maple Character Preview 65

Maple Official Description 65

Kagetsu Character and Romance Details 65

Kagetsu Character Information 66

Character Profile 66

Can You Romance Kagetsu? 67

Will You Romance Kagetsu? 68

Kagetsu Character Preview 68

Kagetsu Official Description 68

Diana Character and Romance Details 68

Diana Character Information 69

Character Profile 69

Can You Romance Diana? 70

Will You Romance Diana? 71

Diana Character Preview 71

Diana Official Description 71

CHAPTER 6: 73

Non-Romanceable Characters 73

Felix Character Guide 73

Felix Character Information 73

Character Profile 73

Felix Character Description 75

Felix Character Preview 75

Felix Official Description 75

Miguel Character Guide 75
Miguel Character Information 76
Character Profile 76
Miguel Character Description 77
Miguel Character Preview 78
Miguel Official Description 78
Erik Character Guide 78
Erik Character Information 79
Character Profile 79
Erik Character Description 80
Erik Character Preview 80
Erik Official Description 80
Stuart Character Guide 80
Stuart Character Information 81
Character Profile 81
Stuart Character Description 82
Stuart Character Preview 83
Stuart Official Description 83
Sonia Character Guide 83
Sonia Character Information 84
Character Profile 84
Sonia Character Description 85
Sonia Character Preview 85
Sonia Official Description 85

STORY OF SEASONS: GRAND BAZAAR

Madeleine Character Guide 85
Madeleine Character Information 86
Character Profile 86
Madeleine Character Description 87
Madeleine Character Preview 88
Madeleine Official Description 88
Mina Character Guide 88
Mina Character Information 89
Character Profile 89
Mina Character Description 90
Mina Character Preview 90
Mina Official Description 90
Wilbur Character Guide 90
Wilbur Character Information 91
Character Profile 91
Wilbur Character Description 92
Wilbur Character Preview 93
Wilbur Official Description 93
Clara Character Guide 93
Clara Character Information 94
Character Profile 94
Clara Character Description 95
Clara Character Preview 95
Clara Official Description 95

Kevin Character Guide 95
Kevin Character Information 96
Character Profile 96
Kevin Character Description 97
Kevin Character Preview 98
Kevin Official Description 98
Isaac Character Guide 98
Isaac Character Information 99
Character Profile 99
Isaac Character Description 100
Isaac Character Preview 101
Isaac Official Description 101
Nadine Character Guide 101
Nadine Character Information 102
Character Profile 102
Nadine Character Description 103
Nadine Character Preview 103
Nadine Official Description 103
Sylvia Character Guide 103
Sylvia Character Information 104
Character Profile 104
Sylvia Character Description 105
Sylvia Character Preview 106
Sylvia Official Description 106

Laurie Character Guide 106

Laurie Character Information 107

Character Profile 107

Laurie Character Description 108

Laurie Character Preview 108

Laurie Official Description 108

CHAPTER 7: 109

Tips and Tricks 109

Marriage Candidates and Benefits 109

Marriage Candidates 109

12 Characters You Can Marry 109

Perks of Marrying in Story of Seasons: Grand Bazaar 111

Allows to Raise Children 111

Unlocks Special Occasions 112

CHAPTER 8: 113

Bazaar 113

Bazaar Guide 113

Bazaar Basics in Story of Seasons: Grand Bazaar 113

Zephyr Town's Own Marketplace 113

Call the Cheer Squad! 114

Opens on Saturdays 116

Nature Sprites Cheer Squad Guide 116

How to Call the Cheer Squad 117

Make Your Customers Happy 117

Press the Cheer Squad Button 118

Who Are the Nature Sprites? 119

Fae-Like Citizens of Zephyr Town 119

How to Sell in the Bazaar 120

How to Sell in the Bazaar 120

Wait for Saturdays 120

Load Up Your Stocks 121

Ring the Bell to Attract Customers 122

Make Your Customers Happy 123

CHAPTER 9: 124

Message Board 124

Questions Board 124

Question Board Rules 124

Discussions Board 125

Discussions Board Rules 126

CHAPTER 1:

All Romance Options: Bachelors and Bachelorettes

There are 12 Bachelors and Bachelorettes you can romance in Story of Seasons: Grand Bazaar.

See a list of all romance options and details about the candidates in the game here!

List of All Bachelors and Bachelorettes

All Bachelors

Character	Harvest Moon Name	Voice Actors
Arata	-	**EN**: Y. Chang **JP**: Daiki Hamano
Derek	Dirk	**EN**: Mark Whitten **JP**: Shoya Chiba
Gabriel	Angelo	**EN**: Kieran Regan **JP**: Wataru Urata

STORY OF SEASONS: GRAND BAZAAR

Jules	Ivan	**EN**: Howard Wang
		JP: Yuma Uchida
Lloyd	Lloyd	**EN**: Daman Mills
		JP: Koki Uchiyama
Samir	Amir	**EN**: Nazeeh Tarsha
		JP: Takeo Otsuka

There are **6 Bachelors** in Story of Seasons: Grand Bazaar. Compared to the Harvest Moon: Grand Bazaar, nearly all of the Romance Options had been given a new name, except for Lloyd who kept his name and **Arata, who is newly added** to the game!

All Bachelorettes

Character	Harvest Moon Name	Voice Actors
Diana	-	EN: Cassie Ewulu JP: Yumiri Hanamori
Freya	Freya	EN: Cat Protano JP: Ai Kakuma
June	Antoinette	EN: Jennifer Losi JP: Maaya Uchida
Kagetsu	Emiko	EN: Anne Yatco

		JP: Megumi Han
Maple	Daisy	**EN**: Madeline Dorroh
		JP: Nao Toyama
Sophie	Sherry	**EN**: Deva Marie Gregory
		JP: Manaka Iwami

There are **6 Bachelorettes** in this game as well, and only Freya got to keep her name from the Harvest Moon: Grand Bazaar.

Similar to Arata, **Diana is new** and unique to the Story of Seasons: Grand Bazaar.

Which Character Do You Want to Date?

Arata	3 Votes
Derek	0 Votes
Diana	1 Votes
Freya	1 Votes
Gabriel	0 Votes
Jules	2 Votes
June	2 Votes
Kagetsu	1 Votes
Lloyd	0 Votes
Maple	0 Votes
Samir	1 Votes
Sophie	0 Votes

Romance in Story of Seasons: Grand Bazaar

Choose From 12 Romance Options

There are **12** characters in Story of Seasons: Grand

Bazaar that players **can romance** throughout their gameplay. Once the right conditions are met, players can **marry their chosen character** and even have a child with them!

Can You Marry the Same Gender?

Yes, players will be able to choose any of the 12 Marriage Options **regardless of the player character's gender**.

Raise Friendship Points to Romance

Players must raise their **Friendship Points** by choosing the right dialogue, completing events, and giving gifts to the character they chose, until you can marry them!

CHAPTER 2:

Can You Marry the Same Gender?

Same gender marriage is allowed in Story of Seasons: Grand Bazaar. Find out the requirements for same gender marriage, if you can have a baby, and other details in this guide!

Can You Marry the Same Gender

Yes, Same Gender Marriage is Allowed

Unlike in the original game, Story of Seasons: Grand Bazaar allows **marriage between characters with the same gender**. The game has

12 romanceable characters: 6 male characters and 6 female characters.

No Changes From Original Game

There are **no additional requirements** for same gender marriage between characters. You only need to meet the **same conditions when marrying a character of a different gender** in the game.

You can also **have a child with your spouse** in game even if both of you are of the same gender.

CHAPTER 3:

List of All Characters

See the list of Story of Seasons: Grand Bazaar characters, including romanceables and other villagers you can befriend in Zephyr Town!

All Characters

List of Romanceable Characters

All Characters

STORY OF SEASONS: GRAND BAZAAR

 **Arata**

 **Derek**

 **Diana**

 **Freya**

 **Gabriel**

 **Jules**

 **June**

 **Kagetsu**

 **Lloyd**

There are **12** characters in Story of Seasons: Grand Bazaar that players **can romance** throughout their gameplay. Once the right conditions are met, players can **marry their chosen character** and even have a child with them!

List of Non-Romanceable Characters

STORY OF SEASONS: GRAND BAZAAR

Isaac   Kevin   Laurie

Madeleine   Miguel   Mina

Nadine   Sonia   Stuart

Sylvia   **Wilbur**

There are other residents of Zephyr Town that have their own roles in the storyline, but are **not romance options**. You can still get to know them and form a friendly bond!

CHAPTER 4:

Bachelors

Jules Character and Romance Details

Jules is a Romanceable Bachelor who you can marry in Story of Seasons: Grand Bazaar. He serves as a tutor and is the older brother of Derek. See Jules' character profile, his official description, voice actors, and other information about him here!

Jules Character Information

Character Profile

Jules		
	Character Type	Bachelor
	Romance Status	Romanceable
	Harvest Moon Name	Ivan
	English Voice Actor	Howard Wang

	Japanese Voice Actor	Yuma Uchida

Can You Romance Jules?

Like in the original DS game, Jules returns as a romanceable character in Story of Seasons: Grand Bazaar!

Will You Romance Jules?

Will definitely romance Jules!	1 Votes
I might romance Jules!	0 Votes
Looking to romance other options!	0 Votes

Jules Character Preview

Jules Official Description

The polite and respectable tutor. Took on the role of guardian for his younger brother, Derek, growing up. Commutes to and from the city.

Derek Character and Romance Details

Derek is a Romanceable Bachelor who you can marry in Story of Seasons: Grand Bazaar. He is an opmistic worker at Café Madeleine and the younger brother of Jules. See Derek's character profile, his official description, voice actors, and other information about him here!

Derek Character Information

Character Profile

Derek		
	**Character Type**	Bachelor
	Romance Status	Romanceable
	Harvest Moon Name	Dirk
	English Voice Actor	Mark Whitten
	Japanese Voice Actor	Shoya Chiba

Can You Romance Derek?

Like in the original DS game, Derek returns as a romanceable character in Story of Seasons: Grand Bazaar!

Will You Romance Derek?

Will definitely romance Derek!	**1** Votes
I might romance Derek!	**0** Votes
Looking to romance other options!	**0** Votes

Derek Character Introduction

Derek seems to have an upper middle class style of clothing on him, which makes his role as a waiter more apparent.

Due to his job putting him in social positions, he has developed a natural sense of charm that is reflected in both his personality and appearance and allows him to converse with almost anyone.

Derek Character Preview

The fun-seeking waiter at Café Madeleine. His optimism, honesty, and charm make it easy for him to hit it off with just about anyone.

Lloyd Character and Romance Details

Lloyd is a Romanceable Bachelor who you can marry in Story of Seasons: Grand Bazaar. He is a smooth-talking traveling merchant. See Lloyd's character profile, his official description, voice actors, and other information about him here!

Lloyd Character Information

Character Profile

Lloyd		
	Character Type	Bachelor
	Romance Status	Romanceable
	Harvest Moon Name	Lloyd

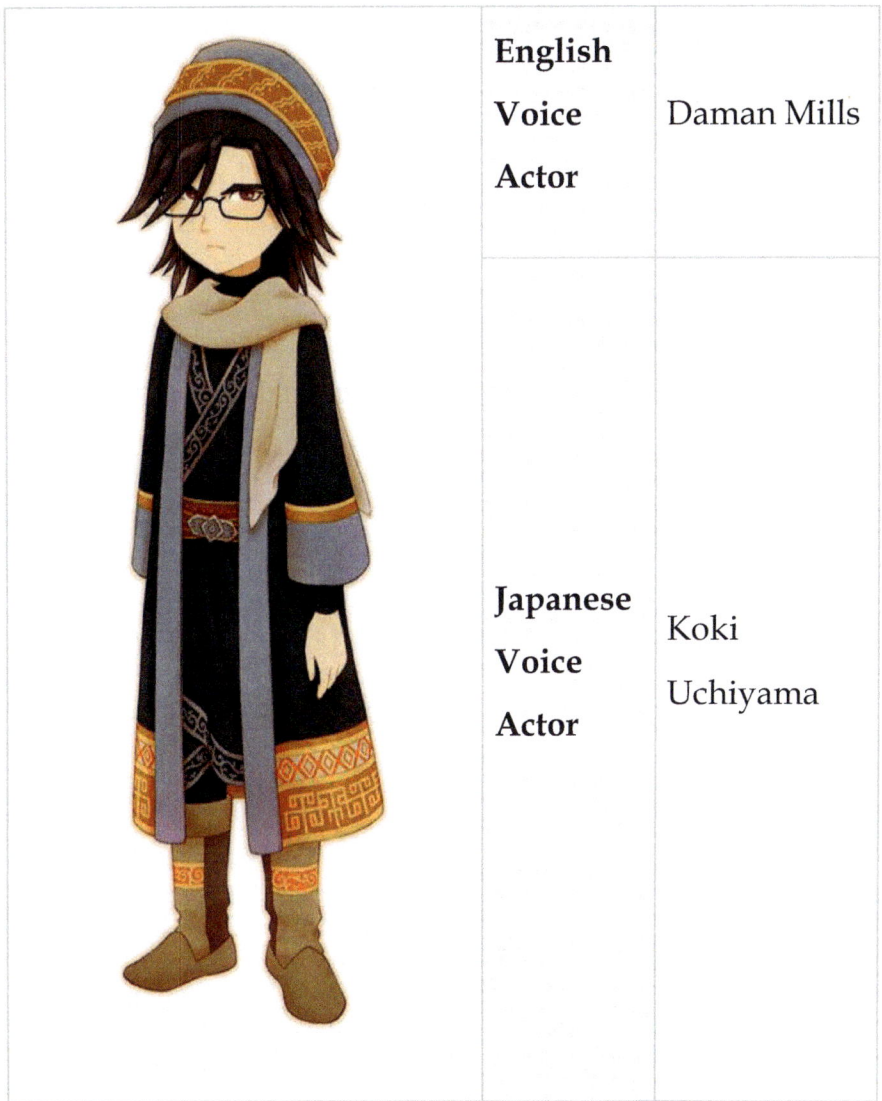	**English Voice Actor**	Daman Mills
	Japanese Voice Actor	Koki Uchiyama

Can You Romance Lloyd?

Like in the original DS game, Lloyd returns as a romanceable character in Story of Seasons: Grand Bazaar!

Will You Romance Lloyd?

Will definitely romance Lloyd!	1 Votes	Vote
I might romance Lloyd!	0 Votes	Vote
Looking to romance other options!	0 Votes	Vote

Lloyd Character Introduction

Lloyd looks to be wearing heavy clothing fit for travel, further solidifying his official description of him being a traveling merchant.

In addition to that, due to his life on the road, he has learned how to temper both himself and other people, and seems to easily be able to negotiate and talk through most obstacles in life.

Lloyd Character Preview

Lloyd Official Description

The traveling merchant temporarily settled in town. His calm, smooth-talker persona has carried him far both in life and business.

Gabriel Character and Romance Details

Gabriel is a Romanceable Bachelor who you can marry in Story of Seasons: Grand Bazaar. He is a carefree artist and a food connoisseur. See Gabriel's character profile, their official description, voice actors, and other information about them here!

Gabriel Character Information

Character Profile

Gabriel	

	Character Type: Bachelor
	Romance Status: Romanceable
	Harvest Moon Name: Angelo
	English Voice Actor: Kieran Regan

	Japanese Voice Actor	Wataru Urata

Can You Romance Gabriel?

Like in the original DS game, Gabriel returns as a romanceable character in Story of Seasons: Grand Bazaar!

Will You Romance Gabriel?

Will definitely romance Gabriel!	1 Votes
I might romance Gabriel!	0 Votes
Looking to romance other options!	0 Votes

Gabriel Character Introduction

Gabriel boasts a freeform and colorful outfit that show off his artistic spirit and way of life.

His general appearance betrays the second part of his official description that denote that he is a food lover.

Gabriel Character Preview

Gabriel Official Description

The carefree, soft-spoken artist. Always carries a sketchbook with him should inspiration strike. A voracious lover of good food.

Samir Character and Romance Details

Samir is a Romanceable Bachelor who you can marry in Story of Seasons: Grand Bazaar. He is a traveler and scholar from abroad with a hidden identity. See Samir's character profile, his official description, voice actors, and other information about him here!

Samir Character Information

Character Profile

Samir		
	Character Type	Bachelor
	Romance Status	Romanceable
	Harvest Moon Name	Amir

English Voice Actor	Nazeeh Tarsha
Japanese Voice Actor	Takeo Otsuka

Can You Romance Samir?

Like in the original DS game, Samir returns as a romanceable character in Story of Seasons: Grand Bazaar!

Will You Romance Samir?

Will definitely romance Samir!	**2** Votes
I might romance Samir!	**0** Votes
Looking to romance other options!	**0** Votes

Samir Character Introduction

Samir seems to be a scholar both based off of his description and his general outfit, which seems different from most of the residents in the town.

It is implied that not many people know about him either due to how little he shares about himself.

Samir Character Preview

HATEM BRYAN MOHAMED

Samir Official Description

The mysterious scholar from abroad. Traveled to see Zephyr Town's bazaar. A man of few words, only the mayor knows his identity.

Arata Character and Romance Details

Arata is a Romanceable Bachelor who you can marry in Story of Seasons: Grand Bazaar. He is a martial artist on a mission of self-improvement. See Arata's character profile, his official description, voice actors, and other information about him here!

Arata Character Information

Character Profile

Arata		
	**Character Type**	Bachelor
	Romance Status	Romanceable
	Harvest Moon Name	N/A
	English Voice Actor	Y. Chang

	Japanese Voice Actor	Daiki Hamano

Can You Romance Arata?

Yes, Arata is a romanceable character in Story of Seasons: Grand Bazaar! He is also a new character that didn't exist in the original DS game.

Will You Romance Arata?

Will definitely romance Arata!	3 Votes
I might romance Arata!	0 Votes
Looking to romance other options!	0 Votes

Arata Character Preview

The martial artist on a journey to better himself.

Tests his strength and skills up in the mountains.

Always offers a friendly grin and a helping hand.

CHAPTER 5:

Bachelorettes

Sophie Character and Romance Details

Sophie is a Romanceable Bachelorette who you can marry in Story of Seasons: Grand Bazaar. She is the mayor's cheerful daughter. See Sophie's character profile, official description, voice actors, and other information about her here!

Sophie Character Information

Character Profile

Sophie

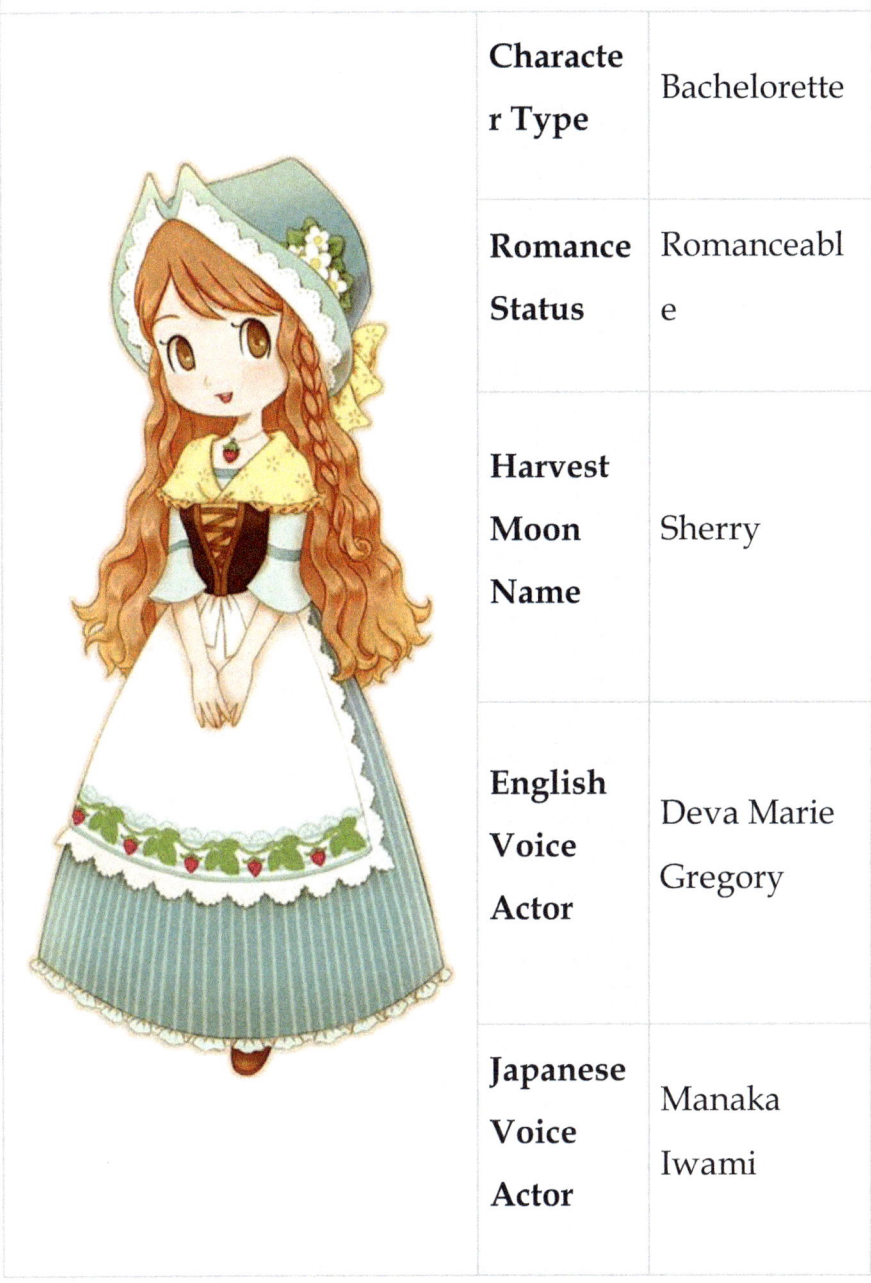

Character Type	Bachelorette
Romance Status	Romanceable
Harvest Moon Name	Sherry
English Voice Actor	Deva Marie Gregory
Japanese Voice Actor	Manaka Iwami

Can You Romance Sophie?

Like in the original DS game, Sophie returns as a romanceable character in Story of Seasons: Grand Bazaar!

Will You Romance Sophie?

Will definitely romance Sophie!	1 Votes
I might romance Sophie!	0 Votes
Looking to romance other options!	0 Votes

Sophie Character Preview

Sophie Official Description

The mayor's bright and cheerful daughter. Dedicates herself to improving her beloved town.

Upbeat and positive no matter how tough things get.

June Character and Romance Details

June is a Romanceable Bachelorette who you can marry in Story of Seasons: Grand Bazaar. She is a talented artisan and new arrival in town. See June's character profile, her official description, voice actors, and other information about her here!

June Character Information

Character Profile

June

Character Type	Bachelorette
Romance Status	Romanceable
Harvest Moon Name	Antoinette
English Voice Actor	Jennifer Losi
Japanese Voice Actor	Maaya Uchida

Can You Romance June?

Like in the original DS game, June returns as a romanceable character in Story of Seasons: Grand Bazaar!

Will You Romance June?

Will definitely romance June!	2 Votes
I might romance June!	0 Votes
Looking to romance other options!	0 Votes

June Character Preview

June Official Description

The new girl in town, recently moved from the city. Appears reticent, but cares deeply for those she trusts. A talented artisan of accessories.

Freya Character and Romance Details

Freya is a Romanceable Bachelorette who you can marry in Story of Seasons: Grand Bazaar. She is a goal-oriented perfectionist. See Freya's character profile, her official description, voice actors, and other information about her here!

Freya Character Information

Character Profile

Freya

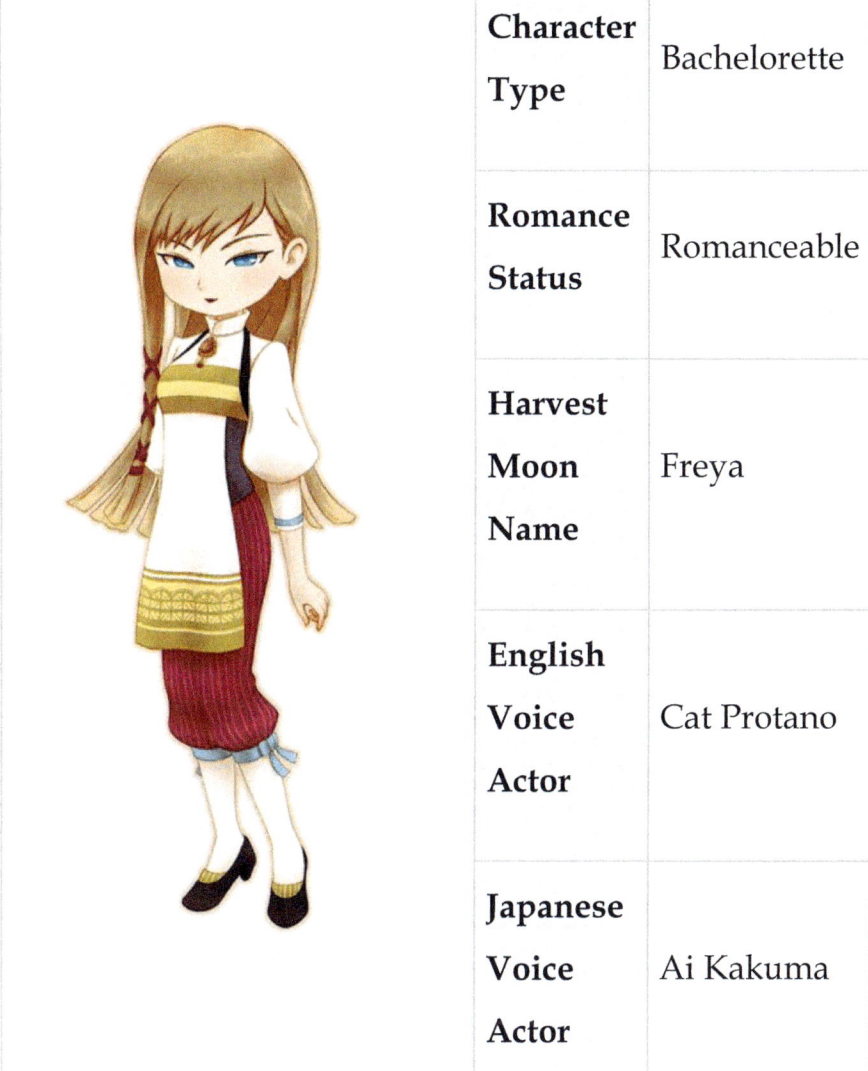

Character Type	Bachelorette
Romance Status	Romanceable
Harvest Moon Name	Freya
English Voice Actor	Cat Protano
Japanese Voice Actor	Ai Kakuma

Can You Romance Freya?

Like in the original DS game, Freya returns as a romanceable character in Story of Seasons: Grand Bazaar!

Will You Romance Freya?

Will definitely romance Freya!	0 Votes	Vote
I might romance Freya!	0 Votes	Vote
Looking to romance other options!	0 Votes	Vote

Freya Character Preview

Freya Official Description

The goal-oriented perfectionist. Likes to stop by the café for a treat on her way home from work in the city. Quick to speak her mind.

Maple Character and Romance Details

Maple is a Romanceable Bachelorette who you can marry in Story of Seasons: Grand Bazaar. She is the maid in Zephyr Town's hotel. See Maple's character profile, her official description, voice actors, and other information about her here!

Maple Character Information

Character Profile

Maple		
	Character Type	Bachelorette

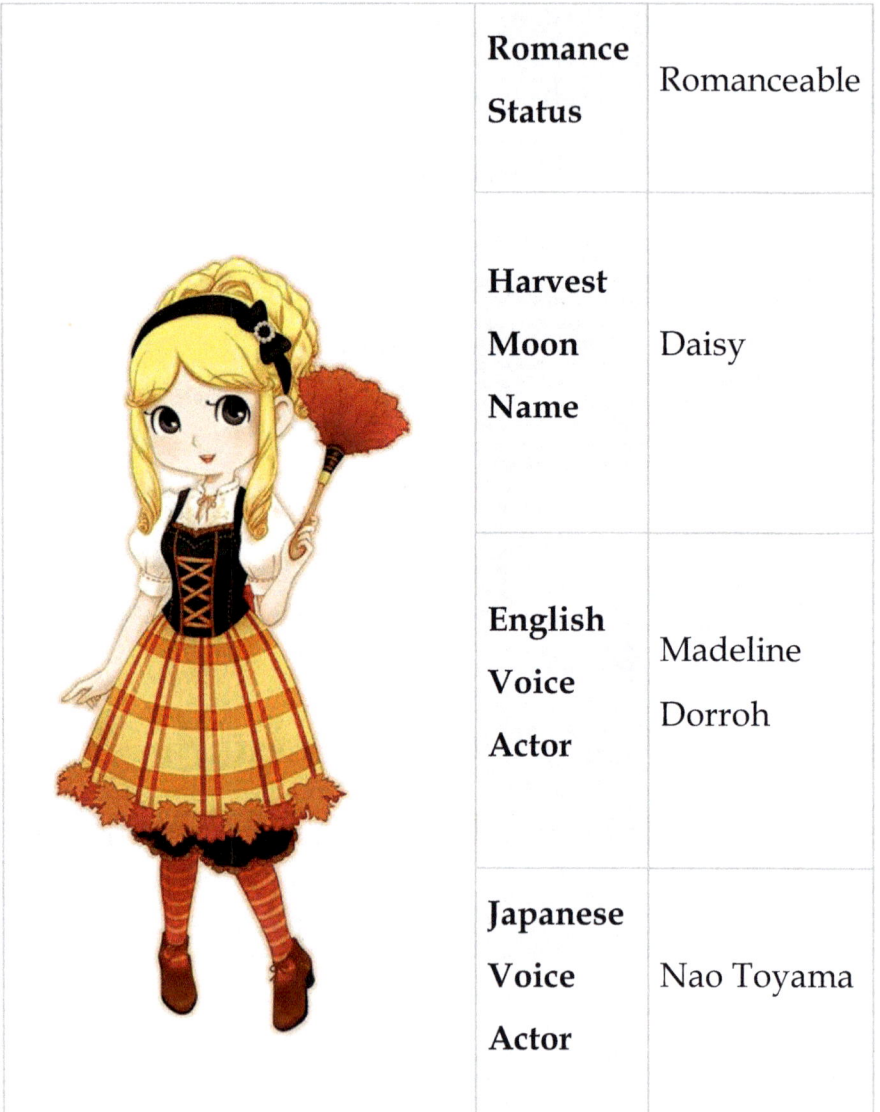	**Romance Status**	Romanceable
	Harvest Moon Name	Daisy
	English Voice Actor	Madeline Dorroh
	Japanese Voice Actor	Nao Toyama

Can You Romance Maple?

Like in the original DS game, Maple returns as a romanceable character in Story of Seasons: Grand Bazaar!

Will You Romance Maple?

Will definitely romance Maple!	**1** Votes
I might romance Maple!	**0** Votes
Looking to romance other options!	**0** Votes

Maple Character Preview

s

Maple Official Description

The bubbly hotel maid. A little overzealous, but shakes mistakes off with a smile. Loves the hotel owners like grandparents.

Kagetsu Character and Romance Details

Kagetsu is a Romanceable Bachelorette who you can marry in Story of Seasons: Grand Bazaar. She is the reclusive shrine maiden. See Kagetsu's character profile, her official description, voice actors, and other information about her here!

Kagetsu Character Information

Character Profile

Kagetsu		
	Character Type	Bachelorette

Romance Status	Romanceable
Harvest Moon Name	Emiko
English Voice Actor	Anne Yatco
Japanese Voice Actor	Megumi Han

Can You Romance Kagetsu?

Like in the original DS game, Kagetsu returns as a romanceable character in Story of Seasons: Grand Bazaar!

Will You Romance Kagetsu?

Will definitely romance Kagetsu!	1 Votes
I might romance Kagetsu!	0 Votes
Looking to romance other options!	0 Votes

Kagetsu Character Preview

Kagetsu Official Description

The mystical, reclusive shrine maiden. Lives in the mountains praying to the spirits who dwell there. Knows little about the outside world.

Diana Character and Romance Details

Diana is a Romanceable Bachelorette who you can marry in Story of Seasons: Grand Bazaar. She is the Bazaar Review Board agent in Zephyr Town. See Diana's character profile, her official description, voice actors, and other information about her here!

Diana Character Information

Character Profile

Diana		
	Character Type	Bachelorette

Romance Status	Romanceable
Harvest Moon Name	N/A
English Voice Actor	Cassie Ewulu
Japanese Voice Actor	Yumiri Hanamori

Can You Romance Diana?

Yes, Diana is a romanceable character in Story of Seasons: Grand Bazaar! She is also a new character that didn't exist in the original DS game.

Will You Romance Diana?

Will definitely romance Diana!	**2** Votes
I might romance Diana!	**0** Votes
Looking to romance other options!	**0** Votes

Diana Character Preview

Diana Official Description

The diligent Bazaar Review Board agent. Focused and clerical, she's all business. Driven to revive the bazaar for personal reasons.

CHAPTER 6:

Non-Romanceable Characters

Felix Character Guide

Felix is a Non-Romanceable NPC in Story of Seasons: Grand Bazaar. He is Zephyr Town's beloved Mayor and Sophie's father. See Felix's character profile, their official description, voice actors, and other information about him here!

Felix Character Information

Character Profile

Felix

Character Type	NPC
Romance Status	Non-Romanceable
Harvest Moon Name	N/A
English Voice Actor	Brent Mukai
Japanese Voice Actor	Hiroki Yasumoto

Felix Character Description

Felix appears to be a man of above-average stature, with a posture that announces his presence.

Towering above most of the town's residents, he is one of Zephyr Town's most prominent figures as the Mayor of the town, and the father of **Sophie**.

Felix Character Preview

Felix Official Description

The hot-blooded town mayor. Works tirelessly to see the bazaar fully restored.

Miguel Character Guide

STORY OF SEASONS: GRAND BAZAAR

Miguel is a Non-Romanceable NPC in Story of Seasons: Grand Bazaar. He is one of three merchants that form a trio in Zephyr Town. See Miguel's character profile, their official description, voice actors, and other information about him here!

Miguel Character Information

Character Profile

Miguel		
	Character Type	NPC
	Romance Status	Non-Romanceable
	Harvest Moon Name	Raul

English Voice Actor	Luis Bermudez
Japanese Voice Actor	Wataru Takagi

Miguel Character Description

Miguel appears to be shorter than most of the residents of Zephyr Town, but stands out with the merchant garbs that he chooses to don.

Miguel Character Preview

Miguel Official Description

One of a trio of merchant brothers. Personable and proud of his business, he loves making a sale.

Erik Character Guide

Erik Character Guide

Erik is a Non-Romanceable NPC in Story of Seasons: Grand Bazaar. He is June's father and a businessman. See Erik's character profile, their official description, voice actors, and other information about them here!

Erik Character Information

Character Profile

Erik		
	Character Type	NPC
	Romance Status	Non-Romanceable
	Harvest Moon Name	Claude
	English Voice Actor	Chris Hackney
	Japanese Voice Actor	Show Hayami

Erik Character Description

Dressed in a dapper suit and maintaining an orderly appearance, Erik gives off an air of class in his general appearance.

This complements both his dedication to **June** as his father, and as an accomplished businessman.

Erik Character Preview

Erik Official Description

The devoted business and family man. Gushes over his daughter, June.

Stuart Character Guide

Stuart is a Non-Romanceable NPC in Story of Seasons: Grand Bazaar. He is the owner of Zephyr Town's hotel, and is Sonia's husband. See Stuart's character profile, their official description, voice actors, and other information about him here!

Stuart Character Information

Character Profile

Stuart		
	Character Type	NPC
	Romance Status	Non-Romanceable
	Harvest Moon Name	N/A

	English Voice Actor	Keith Silverstein
	Japanese Voice Actor	Junpei Morita

Stuart Character Description

Stuart appears to be dressed in clothing that give him comfort throughout the day. This complements his demeanor and role as the jovial hotel manager of Zephyr Town.

Stuart Character Preview

Stuart Official Description

The jovial old man who runs the hotel. Jokes with guests, much to his wife Sonia's chagrin.

Sonia Character Guide

Sonia is a Non-Romanceable NPC in Story of Seasons: Grand Bazaar. She is the other owner of Zephyr Town's hotel, and Stuart's wife. See Sonia's character profile, their official description, voice actors, and other information about her here!

Sonia Character Information

Character Profile

Sonia		
	Character Type	NPC
	Romance Status	Non-Romanceable
	Harvest Moon Name	Ethel
	English Voice Actor	Janis Carroll
	Japanese Voice Actor	Reiko Suzuki

Sonia Character Description

As the Co-Owner of Zephyr Town's hotel, Sonia dresses in a classy but comfortable way that befit her status as the aged Co-Owner.

Sonia Character Preview

Sonia Official Description

The sweet old woman who runs the hotel. Lives a quiet life with her dear husband, Stuart.

Madeleine Character Guide

Madeleine is a Non-Romanceable NPC in Story of Seasons: Grand Bazaar. She is the owner of

Zephyr Town's cafe, and is the grandmother of Mina. See Madeleine's character profile, their official description, voice actors, and other information about her here!

Madeleine Character Information

Character Profile

Madeleine		
	Character Type	NPC
	Romance Status	Non-Romanceable
	Harvest Moon Name	Joan

	English Voice Actor	Rachel Robinson
	Japanese Voice Actor	Kyo Yaoya

Madeleine Character Description

As the owner of Zephyr Town's cafe, Madeleine is dressed in a humble dress along with an apron that shows her profession as the aged and experienced cafe owner.

Madeleine Character Preview

Madeleine Official Description

The spirited owner of the town café. Loves having her granddaughter Mina around.

Mina Character Guide

Mina is a Non-Romanceable NPC in Story of Seasons: Grand Bazaar. She works as a waitress in her grandmother Madeleine's cafe. See Mina's character profile, their official description, voice actors, and other information about them here!

Mina Character Information

Character Profile

Mina		
	Character Type	NPC
	Romance Status	Non-Romanceable
	Harvest Moon Name	Marian
	English Voice Actor	Brianna Knickerbocker
	Japanese Voice Actor	Asami Imai

Mina Character Description

Mina is dressed in the same color-style as her grandmother **Madeleine**, implying that her dress is either a standard attire of the cafe, or that she shares similar outfit choices as her grandmother.

Mina Character Preview

Mina Official Description

The amicable café waitress. Customers flock in daily just to see her. Good friends with Freya.

Wilbur Character Guide

Wilbur is a Non-Romanceable NPC in Story of Seasons: Grand Bazaar. He is Zephyr Town's carpenter, husband to Clara, and the father of Kevin. See Wilbur's character profile, their official description, voice actors, and other information about him here!

Wilbur Character Information

Character Profile

Wilbur		
	Character Type	NPC
	Romance Status	Non-Romanceable
	Harvest Moon Name	N/A

English Voice Actor	Andrew Russell
Japanese Voice Actor	Shinya Fukumatsu

Wilbur Character Description

Wilbur dresses in rather bulky clothing that also helps distinguish his body proportions, which gives off the idea that Wilbur deals in bulky and hard labor, which makes sense given his role as the town's carpenter.

Wilbur Character Preview

Wilbur Official Description

The burly town carpenter and father of Kevin. Gruff, but makes no compromises with his work.

Clara Character Guide

Clara is a Non-Romanceable NPC in Story of Seasons: Grand Bazaar. She is Wilbur's wife and Kevin's mother.

See Clara's character profile, their official description, voice actors, and other information about her here!

Clara Character Information

Character Profile

Clara		
	Character Type	NPC
	Romance Status	Non-Romanceable
	Harvest Moon Name	Claire
	English Voice Actor	Misty Lee
	Japanese Voice Actor	Kana Ueda

Clara Character Description

Clara dresses in a modest way that shows her simple but busy life as a mother.

This outfit also helps her move around the city as it appears perfect for both housework and for outdoor strolls or errands.

Clara Character Preview

Clara Official Description

The gregarious mother. When not wrangling her son, Kevin, she's usually chatting with Nadine.

Kevin Character Guide

Kevin Character Guide

Kevin is a Non-Romanceable NPC in Story of Seasons: Grand Bazaar. He is the son of Wilbur and Clara. See Kevin's character profile, their official description, voice actors, and other information about him here!

Kevin Character Information

Character Profile

Kevin		
	Character Type	NPC
	Romance Status	Non-Romanceable
	Harvest Moon Name	N/A

	English Voice Actor	Melissa Hutchison
	Japanese Voice Actor	Satsumi Matsuda

Kevin Character Description

Kevin seems to be dressed in more comfortable and slightly classier clothing than his parents, indicating that they likely try to spoil him.

This clothing also seems to let him move around quickly, considering his active personality and crafty pastime.

Kevin Character Preview

Kevin Official Description

The mischievous young prankster. Constantly scolded for scheming new tricks.

Isaac Character Guide

Isaac is a Non-Romanceable NPC in Story of Seasons: Grand Bazaar. He is one of Zephyr Town's craftsmen, and is the one responsible for the town windmills. See Isaac's character profile, their official description, voice actors, and other information about him here!

Isaac Character Information

Character Profile

Isaac		
	Character Type	NPC
	Romance Status	Non-Romanceable
	Harvest Moon Name	N/A
	English Voice Actor	Jonathan Lipow

Japanese Voice Actor	Hitoshi Bifu

Isaac Character Description

Isaac dresses in comfortable and fairly wind-resistant clothing as that allows him to perform his work better, considering he is responsible for the maintenance of the town's windmills.

Isaac Character Preview

Isaac Official Description

The craftsman who maintains the town windmills. Father of Sylvia and Laurie, he's got a big heart.

Nadine Character Guide

Nadine is a Non-Romanceable NPC in Story of Seasons: Grand Bazaar. She is the wife of Isaac, and the mother of Sylvia and Laurie. See Nadine's character profile, their official description, voice actors, and other information about her here!

Nadine Character Information

Character Profile

Nadine		
	**Character Type**	NPC
	Romance Status	Non-Romanceable
	Harvest Moon Name	Nellie
	English Voice Actor	Amber Lee Connors
	Japanese Voice Actor	Rika Tachibana

Nadine Character Description

Nadine dresses in what seems to be loose and silky smooth clothing, making her life as a housewife easier.

Nadine Character Preview

Nadine Official Description

The calm, refined housewife. Mother of Sylvia and Laurie, she loves offering good food.

Sylvia Character Guide

Sylvia is a Non-Romanceable NPC in Story of Seasons: Grand Bazaar. She is the extroverted twin sister of Laurie. See Sylvia's character profile, their official description, voice actors, and other information about her here!

Sylvia Character Information

Character Profile

Sylvia		
	Character Type	NPC
	Romance Status	Non-Romanceable
	Harvest Moon Name	Cindy
	English Voice Actor	Dani Chambers

| | Japanese Voice Actor | Honoka Inoue |

Sylvia Character Description

Sylvia, and her more introverted sister **Laurie** by extension, seem to be dressed in the same kind of comfort clothing that their mother **Nadine** wears, indicating that their parents also deeply care for and provide them with the best.

Sylvia Character Preview

Sylvia Official Description

The outgoing twin sister. Her curiosity knows no bounds and she's always eager to talk.

Laurie Character Guide

Laurie is a Non-Romanceable NPC in Story of Seasons: Grand Bazaar. She is the introverted twin sister of Sylvia. See Laurie's character profile, their official description, voice actors, and other information about her here!

Laurie Character Information

Character Profile

Laurie		
	**Character Type**	NPC
	Romance Status	Non-Romanceable
	Harvest Moon Name	Lauren
	English Voice Actor	Ratana
	Japanese Voice Actor	Kokoa Amano

Laurie Character Description

Laurie, and her more outgoing sister **Sylvia** by extension, seem to be dressed in the same kind of comfort clothing that their mother **Nadine** wears, indicating that their parents also deeply care for and provide them with the best.

Laurie Character Preview

Laurie Official Description

The shy twin sister. Comes out of her shell around her sister, Sylvia, and friend, Kevin.

CHAPTER 7:

Tips and Tricks

Marriage Candidates and Benefits

Story of Seasons: Grand Bazaar allows you to choose from 12 marriage candidates to romance. See who they are, how to marry them, and the benefits of marriage in this guide.

Marriage Candidates

12 Characters You Can Marry

Bachelorettes

Sophie	June	Freya
Maple	Kagetsu	Diana

Bachelors

Jules	Derek	Lloyd
Gabriel	Samir	Arata

There are 12 marriage candidates to choose from, including 6 male and 6 female options. Unlike the original DS release, this version allows you to have a relationship and marry any marriage candidate, no matter your character's gender.

Story of Seasons also introduces two new bachelor and bachelorette, **Arata** and **Diana**, who weren't in the previous game!

Perks of Marrying in Story of Seasons: Grand Bazaar

Allows to Raise Children

You can also create your own family after marriage. Watch as your child grow and grow a bigger household!

Recent Story of Seasons games allow adoption of children regardless of your spouse's gender, so we may expect the same for Grand Bazaar!

Unlocks Special Occasions

In the original DS game, marriage unlocks **special celebrations with your spouse**. After getting married, you can celebrate your **wedding anniversary** and the **birthday of your spouse** from the calendar!

CHAPTER 8:

Bazaar

Bazaar Guide

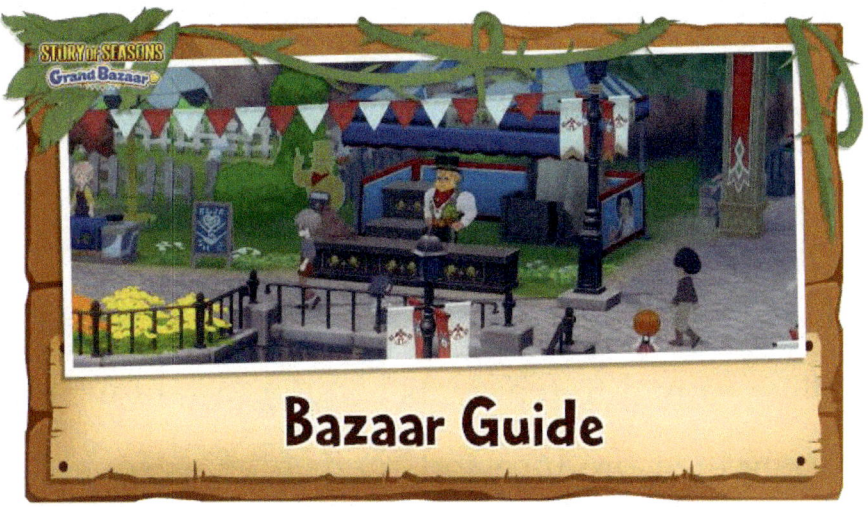

Here's everything you need to know about the Bazaar in Story of Seasons: Grand Bazaar. See what you can do in Zephyr Town's market and all info about it here!

Bazaar Basics in Story of Seasons: Grand Bazaar

Zephyr Town's Own Marketplace

STORY OF SEASONS: GRAND BAZAAR

Set up your own shop!

The Bazaar in Zephyr Town is the town's own local market buzzing with merchants and traders hailing from different walks of life, each of whom, trading their produce and goods for a reasonable amount of gold.

As the new farmer in town, the Bazaar is your prime location when it comes to **selling your crops**, as well as the items you've crafted in the Windmill!

Call the Cheer Squad!

One of the revived gimmicks in Story of Season: Grand Bazaar is the presence of the Nature

Sprites; fae-like residents of the Story of Seasons universe that provide various quality-of-life features to players.

In this iteration of the original DS game, players can call the Nature Sprites, aka the Cheer Squad, to give your shop different buffs to boost your sales, the quality of your items, and more! Players can call the Sprites once the meter located on the upper right portion of the screen is filled to a maximum.

Opens on Saturdays

The Bazaar opens only on Saturdays, giving you, and the locals, ample time to prepare high-quality goodies to make your customers happy! If you're not in the mood to prop up your tent to sell, you can participate in the Bazaar as a customer instead, where you can browse the local stalls, and shop for items that pique your interest!

Nature Sprites Cheer Squad Guide

The Nature Sprites Cheer Squad is a mechanic that provides market buffs to players in Story of

Seasons: Grand Bazaar. See how to trigger the Cheer Squad and all info about it here in this guide!

How to Call the Cheer Squad

Make Your Customers Happy

To trigger the Nature Sprites Cheer Squad, you have to make your customers happy by fulfilling their requests, indicated by the speech bubble hovering above them! Make sure to ace the amount of their orders too, as this contributes more to the Cheer Squad meter!

Press the Cheer Squad Button

Once the Cheer Squad meter is full, press the **Call Cheer Squad** button to call the Nature Sprites. All orders completed and fulfilled during the limited-time buff will have corresponding boosts, such as sales increase and quality increase! Make the most out of this buff to greatly increase your sales!

Keep in mind that you cannot gain charge on the Cheer Squad meter while the buff is active.

Who Are the Nature Sprites?

Fae-Like Citizens of Zephyr Town

The Nature Sprites are locals of Zephyr Town who embody the power of nature. These tiny friends help players increase their sales, and can be spotted on the overworld when the Bazaar is closed!

How to Sell in the Bazaar

You can sell in the Bazaar on Saturdays in Story of Seasons: Grand Bazaar. See how to set up your stall and all info about selling here in this guide!

How to Sell in the Bazaar

Wait for Saturdays

To sell in the Bazaar, you must wait every Saturday since this is the only day when the Bazaar is active. This means that you will have a total of 6 in-game days to prepare your stocks such as crafted items and produce!

Load Up Your Stocks

Before propping up and opening your stall, make sure to load up your stocks! From the official game preview, it looks like the remake has deviated from having to go back and forth your house to access your basket, to simply making everything accessible in your stall. This means that you don't have to momentarily pause your shift just to replenish stocks!

Ring the Bell to Attract Customers

Once you're all prepped up, start your shift and **ring your bell** to garner attention. While you can play passively without ringing your bell, you'll attract more customers if you participate actively, which equates to bigger end-of-day sales and overall profit.

Make Your Customers Happy

A vital part of selling, is making your customers, which you can do by fulfilling their orders correctly. Constantly satisfying your customers also fill up the Cheer Meter gradually, which allows you **call the Nature Sprite Cheer Squad** when maxed out!

CHAPTER 9:

Message Board

Questions Board

Want to ask us or other players something about the Story of Seasons: Grand Bazaar? Use this Questions Board to get the answers to your questions!

Question Board Rules

✿ No submissions that are offensive toward other users.

✿ No slander or harassment.

✿ No posting of images that violate public standards.

✿ No refrain from submissions irrelevant to this board.

✿ No posting of the same contents repeatedly.

✿ No advertising for other sites or apps.

✿ No posting for finanical gain (via RMT, etc.)

Note: If you violate any of these conditions, your submission may be deleted and you may be banned from posting.

Discussions Board

Want to talk about the Story of Seasons: Grand Bazaar? Use this Discussions Board and get the ball rolling!

Discussions Board Rules

✿ No submissions that are offensive toward other users.

✿ No slander or harassment.

✿ No posting of images that violate public standards.

✿ No refrain from submissions irrelevant to this board.

✿ No posting of the same contents repeatedly.

✿ No advertising for other sites or apps.

✿ No posting for finanical gain (via RMT, etc.)

Note: If you violate any of these conditions, your submission may be deleted and you may be banned from posting.

Printed in Dunstable, United Kingdom